The Adventure of Louey and Frank

TEXT BY **CAROLYN WHITE**

PICTURES BY **LAURA DRONZEK**

Greenwillow Books
An Imprint of HarperCollinsPublishers

For the children and
the former children
of Cloghane
—C. W.

For Kevin
—L. D.

Acrylic paints were used for
the full-color art.
The text type is Futura Bold.

The Adventure of Louey and Frank
Text copyright © 2001
by Carolyn White
Illustrations copyright © 2001
by Laura Dronzek
Printed in Hong Kong
by South China Printing
Company (1988) Ltd.
www.harperchildrens.com

Library of Congress
Cataloging-in-Publication Data

White, Carolyn, (date)
The adventure of Louey and Frank /
by Carolyn White ; illustrated by
Laura Dronzek.
    p.   cm.
"Greenwillow Books."
Summary: Two friends, a bear
and a rabbit, build a boat out
of shoes, but after their trip
at sea, the only thing on which
they agree is that their experience
was an adventure.
ISBN 0-688-16503-6 (trade).
ISBN 0-688-16605-9 (lib. bdg.)
[1. Bears—Fiction. 2. Rabbits—Fiction.
3. Friendship—Fiction.
4. Boats and boating—Fiction.]
I. Dronzek, Laura, ill. II. Title.
PZ7.W58248Ad   2001
[E]—dc21   99-038009

10 9 8 7 6 5 4 3 2 1
First Edition

"Let's make a boat," said Louey to Frank.

"Let's sail out to sea," said Frank to Louey.

So Louey and Frank made a boat.

And since they had no wood,

they made a boat out of old shoes.

"We'll tie the shoes together," said Louey.

"We'll use a sock for a sail," said Frank.

And that's what they did.

"I hope the boat floats," said Frank.

"It will," said Louey.

Sure enough, the boat floated.

"I'll bring the pickle sandwiches," said Louey.

"I'll bring the marshmallows," said Frank.

Away they sailed.

Louey waved at the fishes.

Frank tossed marshmallows at the birds.

Ahead they saw something blue and humpy.

It was big.

"It's a rock," said Louey.

"It's a whale," said Frank.

"Phooey," said Louey. "It's a rock, not a whale."

"Rocks don't have tails," said Frank.

"Some rocks do," said Louey.

Louey jumped onto the rock. He was carrying
the bag of marshmallows.

"Bring the pickle sandwiches, Frank," he said.
"Let's have a picnic."

So Frank jumped onto the rock. But he thought
it was a whale.

"It feels like a whale," said Frank. He tapped
his foot.

"Phooey," said Louey. "It feels like a rock."

Frank wasn't sure. Water spouted in the air.

"What luck!" said Louey. "We found a rock with
a geyser."

"That's the whale's blowhole," said Frank.

"Come on, let's toast marshmallows," said Louey.

"Let's build a fire."

"Whales don't like fires," said Frank.

"Rocks do," said Louey. "Rocks like getting hot."

Louey built a fire.

But the rock didn't like getting hot. It rolled.

"Hold on tight," said Louey. "The rock's rocking."

But there was no place to hold on to.

Louey and Frank slid into the sea.

"Save me," cried Louey.

"I can't," said Frank. "Water's in my nose.

I can't see."

So instead of Frank saving Louey, Louey
saved Frank. They climbed onto Louey's
rock that was Frank's whale.

"I saved the marshmallows," said Louey.

"Good," said Frank. "Now save the boat."

The boat bobbed away with the waves.

"Come back, boat," said Louey.

Seagulls flew at the shoelaces. Sharks chewed
on the shoes. The boat fell apart.
"Kablooey," said Louey. "What shall we do?"
"Let's feed the whale marshmallows and
coax it to carry us home," said Frank.

"Don't be screwy," said Louey.
"Rocks don't eat marshmallows.
Help me roll this rock
to the shore."
So while Frank fed the whale,
Louey rolled the rock with his feet
until there sprang up a storm.

"It's raining," said Frank.

"The rock's sinking," said Louey.

"We're going down," said Frank.

"This is the end," said Louey.

"Good-bye, friend," said Frank.

Louey and Frank sank into the sea

and were hurled about by the storm.

"What's this?" said Louey.

"It's a log," said Frank.

"It's got prickers," said Louey. "It's a fish."

"Climb on quick," said Frank.

"I wish this fish didn't wiggle," said Louey.

"Sit still," said Frank. "It's a log."

The friends huddled together.

They heard thunder. They saw lightning.

"This is fun," said Louey.

"Phooey," said Frank.

"The storm's stopping," said Louey.

"I see the shore," said Frank.

"I'm hungry. Where are the marshmallows?"
said Louey.

"The whale ate them," said Frank.

"Whales don't eat marshmallows," said Louey.

"Besides, the whale was a rock."

"It was a whale," said Frank.

"It was a rock," said Louey.

"It was a whale," said Frank.

"It was an adventure," said Louey.

"It was an adventure," Frank agreed.

And they went home to eat peanut

butter and honey.